Other books written and illustrated by David Small

Paper John

Fenwick's Suit

Books by Sarah Stewart
Illustrated by David Small

The Money Tree

The Library

The Gardener

George Washington's Cows

David Small

Farrar Straus Giroux

New York

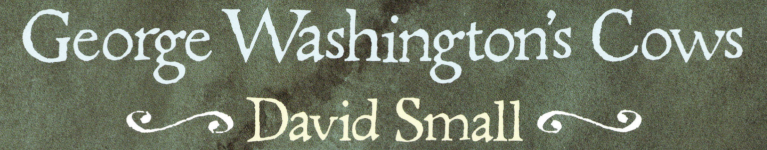

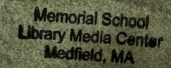

To Sarah and Mark

Special thanks to the Mount Vernon Ladies Association

Library of Congress Cataloging-in-Publication Data. Small, David. George Washington's cows /
David Small.— 1st ed. p. cm. [1. Washington, George, 1732–1799—Fiction. 2. Domestic
animals—Fiction. 3. Stories in rhyme.] I. Title. PZ8.3.S634Ge 1994 [E]—dc20 93-39989 CIP AC
ISBN-13: 978-0-374-42534-0 (pbk.) / ISBN-10: 0-374-42534-5 (pbk.)

George Washington's cows were kept upstairs
And given their own special room.

They never were seen by the light of day,
No matter for what or by whom.

They had to be dressed in lavender gowns
and bedded on cushions of silk,

Fed on a diet of jam and cream scones,
Frequently sprayed with expensive colognes,
Begged every hour in obsequious tones,
Or they just wouldn't give any milk.

George Washington's hogs, on the other hand,
Were a genteel and amiable group,

Delighted to help with the household chores
If a servant had fever or croup.

They served the dinner precisely at eight
With manners uncommonly fine.

Eager to serve the honored guests,
Leaping to meet each need expressed,
Always polite and impeccably dressed,
They were certainly well-bred swine.

George Washington's sheep were all scholars,
With a flock of impressive degrees.

They had not the least bit of trouble
In counting to twenty by threes.

They sorted the stars with a needle
And measured the sea with a stick.

Then, raising their hoofs in triumph, they cried:
"We say with a certain amount of pride,
If the ocean were stood up on its side
You would see that it's deep but not thick!"

A.

B.

Deep
(not thick)

With head in hand, George Washington sighed
And shed a few tears in his tea.

"My cows wear dresses, my pigs wear wigs,
And my sheep are more learnèd than me.
In all my days on the farm I've seen
Nothing to equal such tricks."

Then bundling into his wool underwear,
He ferried across the cold Delaware,
And muttered in tones of deepest despair: